D0552057

Charlie's PE Kit

Written by Barbara Miller

Illustrated by Louise Ellis

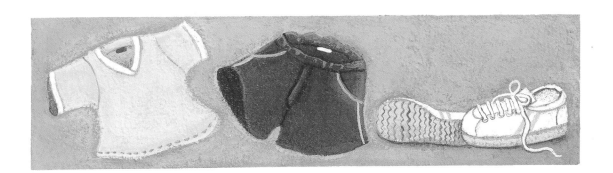

"Mum, where's my T-shirt?"
said Charlie.
"Where did you leave it?"
said Mum.

He looked on the chair.

"Now I remember," he said.

He put it in his bag.

"Mum, where are my shorts?"
said Charlie.
"Where did you leave them?"
said Mum.

He looked under the bed.

"Now I remember," he said.

He put them in his bag.

"Mum, where are my trainers?"
said Charlie.
"Where did you leave them?"
said Mum.
He looked on the chair.
"There they are...

...no, not there!"

He looked under the bed.

"There they are...

...no, not there!"

Charlie looked and looked and looked.

"Now I remember!" he said.

"Here they are, in my bag!"